This
PJ BOOK
belongs to

_____

_____

PJ Library®

JEWISH BEDTIME STORIES and SONGS

How to Heal a Broken Wing

How to Heal a Bro

ken Wing   BOB GRAHAM

High above the city,

no one heard the soft thud of feathers against glass.

No one saw the bird fall.

No one looked down . . .

except Will.

Will saw a bird with a broken wing . . .

and he took it home.

A loose feather can't be put back . . .

but a broken wing can sometimes heal.

With rest . . .

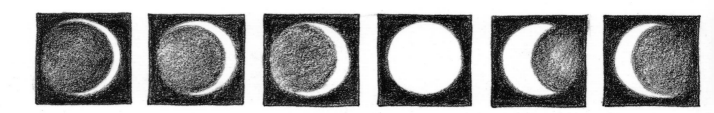

and time . . .

and a little hope . . .

a bird may fly again.

Will opened his hands . . .

and with a beat of its wings,
the bird was gone.

For Lyndsay and Ella

With thanks to Rosie for her fabulous title lettering

First U.S. edition 2008

This edition published specially for the PJ Library®/
The Harold Grinspoon Foundation 2014 by Candlewick Press

Library of Congress Cataloging-in-Publication Data

Graham, Bob, date.
How to heal a broken wing / Bob Graham. — 1st U.S. ed.
p.   cm.
Summary: When Will finds a bird with a broken wing, he takes it home
and cares for it, hoping in time that it will be able to return to the sky.
ISBN 978-0-7636-3903-7 (Candlewick hardcover edition)
[1. Birds — Fiction. 2. Healing — Fiction.]   I. Title.
PZ7.G751667Ho 2008
[E] — dc22   2007040622

ISBN 978-0-7636-7547-9 (Harold Grinspoon paperback edition)

copyright code: 061419K1

14 15 16 17 18 19 TWPS 10 9 8 7 6 5 4 3 2 1

Printed in Singapore

This book was typeset in Stempel Schneidler Light.
The illustrations were done in pen, watercolor, and chalk.

Candlewick Press
99 Dover Street
Somerville, Massachusetts 02144

visit us at www.candlewick.com

Bob Graham is the author-illustrator of many acclaimed books for children, including *"Let's Get a Pup!" Said Kate,* winner of a *Boston Globe–Horn Book* Award, and its sequel, *"The Trouble with Dogs . . ." Said Dad.* His other titles include *Max, Oscar's Half Birthday,* and *Dimity Dumpty.*

About this book, he says, "In troubled times, when many of us are losing contact with the natural world, I wanted to show that there is still hope in a coming generation of children who have curiosity and empathy with the world around them, and that care and attention can sometimes fix broken wings." Bob Graham lives in Australia.